MW01199104

PRESIDENTS

GEORGE W. BUSH

A MyReportLinks.com Book

Tim O'Shei & Joe Marren

MyReportLinks.com Books

an imprint of

 Enslow Publishers, Inc.

Box 398, 40 Industrial Road
Berkeley Heights, NJ 07922
USA

MyReportLinks.com Books, an imprint of Enslow Publishers, Inc. MyReportLinks®
is a registered trademark of Enslow Publishers, Inc.

Library of Congress Cataloging-in-Publication Data

O'Shei, Tim.
  George W. Bush : a MyReportLinks.com book / Tim O'Shei & Joe Marren.
      p. cm.—(presidents)
Summary: A biography of George Walker Bush, who was inaugurated
president of the United States in 2001. Includes Internet links to Web
sites, source documents, and photographs related to George W. Bush.
Includes bibliographical references and index.
  ISBN 0-7660-5133-1
  1. Bush, George W. (George Walker), 1946– ——Juvenile literature. 2.
Presidents—United States—Biography—Juvenile literature. [1. Bush,
George W. (George Walker), 1946– 2. Presidents.] I. Marren, Joe. II.
Title.
  E903.O84 2003
  973.931'092—dc21

                              2003006031

Printed in the United States of America

10 9 8 7 6 5 4 3 2

To Our Readers:
Through the purchase of this book, you and your library gain access to the Report Links that specifically back
up this book.
The Publisher will provide access to the Report Links that back up this book and will keep these Report Links
up to date on **www.myreportlinks.com** for five years from the book's first publication date.
We have done our best to make sure all Internet addresses in this book were active and appropriate when we
went to press. However, the author and the Publisher have no control over, and assume no liability for, the
material available on those Internet sites or on other Web sites they may link to.
The usage of the MyReportLinks.com Books Web site is subject to the terms and conditions stated on the
Usage Policy Statement on **www.myreportlinks.com**.
A password may be required to access the Report Links that back up this book. The password is found on
the bottom of page 4 of this book.
Any comments or suggestions can be sent by e-mail to comments@myreportlinks.com or to the address on
the back cover.

Photo Credits: AP/Wide World Photos, pp. 11, 14, 21, 29, 43, 44; British Broadcasting Corporation
© 2002–2003, p. 13; © Corel Corporation, p. 3; © Copyright 1999 The Washington Post Company,
p. 19; Copyright © 2003 MacNeil/Lehrer Productions, p. 32; Copyright © 2002 Time Inc., p. 40;
Department of Defense, www.defenselink.mil, photo by Erik Draper, p. 1; George Bush Presidential
Library, pp. 17, 25; MyReportLinks.com Books, p. 4; Texas State Library & Archives Commission,
pp. 24, 27; White House, pp. 23, 34, 36.

Cover Photo: © Corel Corporation; Department of Defense, www.defenselink.mil, photo by Erik Draper.

Contents

MyReportLinks.com Books
Great Books, Great Links, Great for Research!

MyReportLinks.com Books present the information you need to learn about your report subject. In addition, they show you where to go on the Internet for more information. The pre-evaluated Report Links that back up this book are kept up to date on **www.myreportlinks.com**. With the purchase of a MyReportLinks.com Books title, you and your library gain access to the Report Links that specifically back up that book. The Report Links save hours of research time and link to dozens—even hundreds—of Web sites, source documents, and photos related to your report topic.

Please see "To Our Readers" on the Copyright page for important information about this book, the MyReportLinks.com Books Web site, and the Report Links that back up this book.

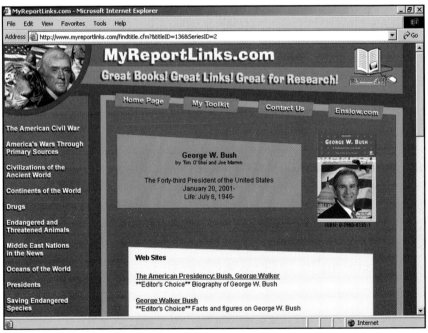

Access:

The Publisher will provide access to the Report Links that back up this book and will try to keep these Report Links up to date on our Web site for five years from the book's first publication date. Please enter **PWB7726** if asked for a password.

Report Links

The Internet sites described below can be accessed at
http://www.myreportlinks.com

*EDITOR'S CHOICE

▶ **The American Presidency: George W. Bush**
The American Presidency Web site provides a history of George
W. Bush's early political career and the presidential election of 2000.

Link to this Internet site from http://www.myreportlinks.com

*EDITOR'S CHOICE

▶ **George Walker Bush**
Internet Public Library Web site provides facts and figures about
George W. Bush. Here you will find election results, historical
documents,
and media resources.

Link to this Internet site from http://www.myreportlinks.com

*EDITOR'S CHOICE

▶ **America's Day of Terror**
At this BBC News Web site you can explore the events of September
11, 2001. Here you will learn about the hijackers and the World Trade
Center, and you can view a time line of events. You can also view
images and read eyewitness accounts.

Link to this Internet site from http://www.myreportlinks.com

*EDITOR'S CHOICE

▶ **"I Do Solemnly Swear . . ."**
At this Library of Congress Web site you can explore George W. Bush's
inauguration through images of the ceremony and the text of his
inaugural address.

Link to this Internet site from http://www.myreportlinks.com

*EDITOR'S CHOICE

▶ **America At War**
At the *Time for Kids Online* Web site you can explore current events
regarding the war in Iraq. Here you will learn about key players, Iraq
and its neighboring countries, and the armed forces.

Link to this Internet site from http://www.myreportlinks.com

*EDITOR'S CHOICE

▶ **George W. Bush (2001–present)**
At the American President Web site you will find a comprehensive
biography of George W. Bush. Here you will learn about his early years
and presidential years. You will also learn about the first lady, his
cabinet, staff and advisors, and key events in his administration.

Link to this Internet site from http://www.myreportlinks.com

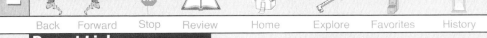

The Internet sites described below can be accessed at
http://www.myreportlinks.com

▶ **The American Presidency: Bush, George Herbert Walker**
The forty-first president of the United States, George H. W. Bush, is also
the father of President George W. Bush. At the American Presidency Web site
you can read his biography and learn about his early life, political career,
and presidency.

Link to this Internet site from http://www.myreportlinks.com

▶ **American Presidents: George W. Bush**
The American Presidents Web site provides information about George W. Bush.
Here you will find "Life Facts" and "Did you know?" trivia. You will also find
links to his inaugural address and birthplace.

Link to this Internet site from http://www.myreportlinks.com

▶ **Bush: The Making of a Candidate**
From the *Washington Post* Web site you will find several articles related to
George W. Bush and his rise to presidency. Some articles discuss challenges
Bush faced, his college years, and his purchase of the Texas Rangers.

Link to this Internet site from http://www.myreportlinks.com

▶ **Donald H. Rumsfeld: Secretary of Defense**
The U.S. Department of Defense Web site holds a brief biography of
Donald Rumsfeld, the United States secretary of defense. Here you will
learn basic facts about his life and political career.

Link to this Internet site from http://www.myreportlinks.com

▶ **Election 2000**
At this CNN Web site you can explore the 2000 election. Here you will
find images, statistics, articles, presidential facts, and much more.

Link to this Internet site from http://www.myreportlinks.com

▶ **Famous Texans: George Walker Bush**
At the Famous Texans Web site you will find a brief profile on George W. Bush.
Here you will learn about his life, education, family, profession, and career.

Link to this Internet site from http://www.myreportlinks.com

Report Links

 The Internet sites described below can be accessed at
http://www.myreportlinks.com

▶*Frontline:* **The Choice 2000**
This PBS Web site for the series *Frontline* explores the politics of
presidential candidates George W. Bush and Al Gore in the year
2000 election. Here you can read interviews and view short videos
of monumental moments in both candidates' lives.
Link to this Internet site from http://www.myreportlinks.com

▶ **George W. Bush: Fifty-Fifth Inaugural Ceremony**
From the White House Web site, you can read President Bush's second
inaugural address from January 2005.
Link to this Internet site from http://www.myreportlinks.com

▶ **Inauguration 2001**
At this PBS Web site you can explore George W. Bush's first
Inauguration Day. Find out about inauguration fashion, history,
and take a presidential quiz.
Link to this Internet site from http://www.myreportlinks.com

▶ **The Laura Bush Foundation for American Libraries**
At the Laura Bush Foundation for American Libraries, you can learn
about the foundation's goals and read remarks made by Laura Bush.
Link to this Internet site from http://www.myreportlinks.com

▶ **The Life of George W. Bush**
The *Washington Post* Web site provides a brief history of the life of
George W. Bush. Learn about his early years, school days, family life,
and public life.
Link to this Internet site from http://www.myreportlinks.com

▶ **Objects From the Presidency**
By navigating through this Web site you will find objects related to all
United States presidents, including George W. Bush. Find out about
the Bush administration and the office of the presidency.
Link to this Internet site from http://www.myreportlinks.com

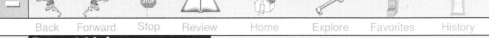
Report Links

The Internet sites described below can be accessed at
http://www.myreportlinks.com

▶ **The Official Site of the Texas Rangers**
In 1989, George Bush became a managing partner of the Texas Rangers
baseball team. At the official Texas Rangers Web site you can explore the
history of the team.

Link to this Internet site from http://www.myreportlinks.com

▶ **Portraits of Texas Governors**
At the Texas State Library & Archives Commission you will find brief profile
of former Texas governors Ann Richards and George W. Bush. Bush ran against
Ann Richards in 1994 as the Republican nominee for governor and won.

Link to this Internet site from http://www.myreportlinks.com

▶ **President Bush: September 11, 2001**
Online News Hour provides the text to George W. Bush's address to the
nation after the September 11 attack on America. You will also find other
links related to September 11 at this site.

Link to this Internet site from http://www.myreportlinks.com

▶ **Secretary of State Condoleeza Rice**
At the U.S. Department of State Web site you can read the biography of
Condoleeza Rice. You can also learn about Rice's travels, view a photo gallery,
and more.

Link to this Internet site from http://www.myreportlinks.com

▶ **U.S. Department of Homeland Security**
The U.S. Department of Homeland Security was created under the
Bush administration as a result of the September 11 attacks on America.
The U.S. Department of Homeland Security Web site provides access to
information regarding threat advisories and what to do in emergencies.
Link to this Internet site from http://www.myreportlinks.com

▶ **The War Behind Closed Doors**
At this PBS Web site, the *Frontline* series explores George W. Bush's
decision to go to war with Iraq. Here you will find opinions, interviews,
and chronology of events leading up to the "Bush Doctrine."

Link to this Internet site from http://www.myreportlinks.com

The Internet sites described below can be accessed at
http://www.myreportlinks.com

▶**The White House: Barbara Pierce Bush**
The official White House Web site holds the biography of the former
first lady, and mother of George W. Bush. Here you will learn about
Barbara Bush's life and experiences in the White House.

Link to this Internet site from http://www.myreportlinks.com

▶**The White House: President George W. Bush**
At the official White House Web site you can explore current
events, life in the White House, and current policies.

Link to this Internet site from http://www.myreportlinks.com

▶**The White House: The Office of Laura Bush**
At the official White House Web site you can explore the life of
Laura Bush. Here you will find speeches given by the first lady
and learn about projects she is working on. You will also find
photographs and essays.

Link to this Internet site from http://www.myreportlinks.com

▶**The White House: The Office of the Vice President**
The official White House Web site holds the biography of Vice
President Richard Cheney. You will also find links to speeches and
news regarding the vice president as well as photographs and essays.

Link to this Internet site from http://www.myreportlinks.com

▶**Why Afghanistan?**
At the *Time for Kids Online* Web site you can read an article
discussing how Afghanistan became the United States' main
focus after the September 11 attacks on America.

Link to this Internet site from http://www.myreportlinks.com

▶***World Almanac for Kids Online:* George W. Bush**
The *World Almanac for Kids Online* Web site holds a brief overview of
George W. Bush. Here you will learn about Bush's early career, the
2000 election, his presidency, and September 11.

Link to this Internet site from http://www.myreportlinks.com

Highlights

1946—*July 6:* George W. Bush born in New Haven, Connecticut.

1953—*Oct. 11:* Younger sister, Robin, dies of leukemia.

1968—Graduates with a B.A. degree from Yale University.

1973—Leaves the Texas Air National Guard to go to graduate school.

1975—Earns an MBA from Harvard University.

1975–1986—Involved in the oil and natural gas business in West Texas.

1977—*Nov. 5:* Marries Laura Welch.

1977—Forms oil exploration company.

1978—Runs unsuccessfully for the U.S. House of Representatives.

1981—*Nov. 25:* Becomes the father of twin girls, Barbara and Jenna.

1988—*Nov. 8:* Father elected president of the United States. George W. Bush was an adviser and speechwriter in the race.

1989–1994—Moves back to Texas and becomes managing partner of the Texas Rangers of Major League Baseball.

1992—*Nov. 3:* Father loses presidential reelection bid to Bill Clinton. George W. Bush again helped with the campaign.

1994—*Nov. 8:* Elected governor of Texas.

1998—*Nov. 3:* Reelected governor of Texas.

1999—Announces in Des Moines, Iowa, that he is officially a candidate for president.

2000—*Nov. 7:* Elected president of the United States. Disputed results cause outcome to not be determined until December 12.

2001—*Jan. 20:* George W. Bush is sworn in as the forty-third president.

—*Sep. 11:* Terrorists attack World Trade Center and Pentagon.

—*Nov. 13:* President issues military order and sends troops to Afghanistan.

2003—*March 19:* Operation Iraqi Freedom begins.

2004—Bush is reelected to another four-year term.

Chapter 1

A Day Like No Other:
September 11, 2001

The morning of September 11, 2001, started out like any other for George W. Bush. The president was on one of his many trips, this one to Florida. The evening before, he had enjoyed dinner with his brother, Florida Governor Jeb Bush, along with a few friends.

Now, the next morning, the president awoke while most of the world was still asleep. Around 6:00 A.M., he went for a four-mile run through the golf course at the Florida resort where he was staying.

At the same time, nineteen men began to execute their evil plan.

▲ A second plane crashed into the south tower of the World Trade Center at 9:03 A.M. EDT, eighteen minutes after the first plane collided into the north tower. The 110-story towers collapsed in the most devastating terrorist attack ever on America.

At 8:30 A.M., Bush's motorcade left for Emma E. Booker Elementary School, where he was scheduled to read to a class of second graders and announce a new nationwide education program. Of course, the president did not know it at the time, but those nineteen men had each boarded airliners in northern cities. Within moments, they would be acting as passengers and reveal themselves as hijackers. They were spread across four different planes, each destined for doom.

▶ Class Interrupted

As President Bush and his staff arrived at the school, news came that a plane had crashed into the north tower of the World Trade Center in New York City. At first, the president and his staff assumed it had been a small plane flown by one pilot who made a terrible error. "I thought it was an accident, I thought it was a pilot error," he said later. "I thought that some foolish soul had gotten lost and made a terrible mistake."[1]

Soon, however, they would learn that this was no small plane and no small mistake. As Bush was sitting with Ms. Kay Daniels's second-grade class, his press secretary, Ari Fleischer, received a message on his pager that the south tower had been hit. The president's chief of staff, Andrew Card, walked up and whispered the news in his ear: "A second plane hit the second tower. America is under attack."[2]

Though the president remained in front of the class for another few moments, his mind had drifted elsewhere. He noticed that the reporters in the back of the classroom were getting phone calls and pager messages. The president saw the worried looks on their faces, and on those of his staff. Later, in interviews, he admitted to thinking at that exact moment that America was going to war. The world he knew had exploded—almost literally—in New York City that day.

As Bush said good-bye to the class, a reporter called out, "Mr. President, are you aware of reports of the plane crash in New York? And is there anything—" Bush nodded and put up his hand, signaling reporters to ask no more questions. "I'll talk about it later," he said.[3]

Readying for War

The president retreated to his "holding room," which was actually a classroom that had been set up with secure

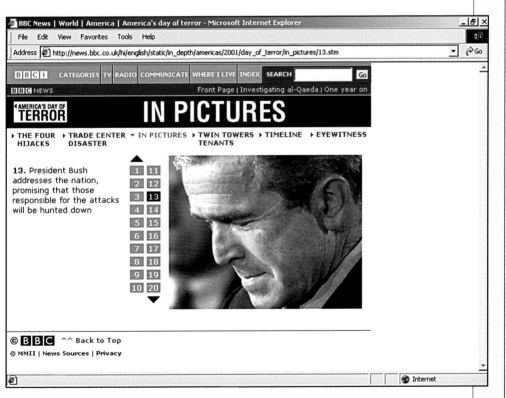

▲ Soon after the attacks on America on September 11, 2001, a saddened George W. Bush addressed the nation. He assured American citizens that the hijackers would be caught.

▲ *When hijackers crashed American Airlines flight 77 into the Pentagon, 229 people were killed—165 in the government building and the 64 passengers aboard the plane.*

phone lines and other communications equipment. He talked to Vice President Richard Cheney, New York Governor George Pataki, and FBI Director Robert Mueller on the telephone while watching news coverage of the World Trade Center attacks on television. Using a yellow legal pad, Bush wrote some words he wanted to share with the nation.

At 9:30 A.M., Bush stepped to a podium at the school and addressed the nation. "Ladies and gentlemen," he said, "this is a difficult moment for America." The president went on to explain that two airplanes had crashed into the World Trade Center "in an apparent terrorist attack on our country." He then added the words that would define the remainder of his presidency: "Terrorism against our nation will not stand."[4]

Within a half hour, the president was leaving Florida aboard *Air Force One*. Meanwhile, another plane crashed into the Pentagon, the United States military headquarters in Washington, D.C. A fourth plane also appeared to be headed for the nation's capital—possibly toward the White House or Capitol Building—but crashed into a field in Pennsylvania. Later, it was learned that some passengers fought the hijackers and brought down the plane.

Air Force One took the president to Barksdale Air Force Base in Louisiana, where he kept in communication with the vice president and his other advisers. He had wanted to return to Washington right away but was told it was unsafe. Amid all the confusion, some people had even suspected *Air Force One* might be a target. The Secret Service was not going to take chances with the president's life.

▶ Back Home

By early evening, however, the president decided to return to the White House anyhow. At 6:34 P.M., *Air Force One* landed at Andrews Air Force Base in Maryland. The president's helicopter took him back to the White House— but not before flying over the Pentagon so Bush could see the damage.

Back at the White House, the president prepared to make a formal, seven-minute address to the nation from his desk in the Oval Office. "Good evening," he said. "Today our fellow citizens, our way of life, our very freedom came under attack in a series of deliberate and deadly terrorist attacks . . ."[5]

From the information Bush had, he thought the person behind the attacks was Osama bin Laden, leader of the al Qaeda terrorist network. Bush had already decided that the United States was going to war against terrorism. "We will make no distinction," he said, "between the terrorists who committed these acts and those who harbor them."[6]

Chapter 2

Successful Young Family, 1946–1964

George Walker Bush was born into a world of politics and power. He had the same name, went to the same schools, and even held the some of the same jobs as his famous father.

When George W. Bush was born on July 6, 1946, in New Haven, Connecticut, he was the first child of George Herbert Walker Bush and the former Barbara Pierce. At the time, George W.'s father was majoring in economics at Yale University.

The elder George Bush had been the Navy's youngest pilot in World War II. After he was shot down over the Pacific Ocean by the Japanese but courageously survived, he became a war hero. Barbara Bush was the daughter of Marvin Pierce, a successful publisher in New York City.

After Bush graduated from Yale, he moved his family to west Texas and entered the oil business. They lived in a two-room apartment that was so small that they had to share a bathroom with another family.

As George W.'s dad worked his way up in the oil business, the family grew too. In 1949, when the Bushes were living in California, daughter Robin (Pauline Robinson Bush) was born. Their third child, Jeb, was born back in Texas in 1953.

▶ Losing Robin

By the time Jeb was born, the Bushes were a happy and successful young family. George Bush was working hard and moving up in the oil business; Barbara Bush stayed home and was close with her children.

All that happiness was wiped out just a few weeks after Jeb's birth. Robin woke up one day and said, "I don't know what to do this morning. I may go out and lie on the grass and watch the cars go by, or I might just stay in bed."[1]

Barbara Bush was alarmed that her three-year-old would say something so unusual, so she took Robin to see a doctor. After testing the little girl, the doctor met Barbara and George Bush and delivered crushing news: Robin had leukemia, an incurable and deadly blood disease. Their little girl had only weeks, maybe months, to live.

George W. Bush was the first child of George Herbert Walker Bush and Barbara Pierce Bush.

George and Barbara decided not to tell "Georgie" that his little sister was sick. For much of the next six months, Barbara and Robin lived in New York City, where the little girl was treated at a hospital. Georgie and Jeb stayed with friends, and their father flew back and forth between New York and Texas.

One day in October, George—now in second grade—was walking through the hallway in his school when he noticed his parents' car outside. They had come to deliver the bad news: Robin had died.

Adults who knew the Bush family at the time remember Georgie keeping his spirits high. Once, when a friend called him on the phone and asked him to play, George said he could not. He had to stay home and take care of his mother.

Friends remember Georgie always playing the clown and cheering up his mother, but he recalls it differently: "I don't remember much of that," he wrote in his autobiography, *A Charge to Keep*. "I remember being sad."[2]

▶ A Special High School

George and Barbara Bush had three more children: Neil, Marvin, and Dorothy. The family moved to Houston when George W. was in middle school, but he did not stay in the big Texas city for long. When George W. turned fifteen, his mom and dad sent him to an elite preparatory school that his father had also attended—Phillips Academy, in Andover, Mass. They wanted their son to receive the same high-class education and, by living on his own, gain the maturity that comes with independence.

When George W.'s father attended Phillips, his grades placed him at the top of his class. George W.'s grades were not nearly as good—he was average at best—but he was popular among his classmates. He was the football team's head cheerleader, and he started a stickball league, appointing himself commissioner.

Yale-bound

After graduating from Andover in 1964, George flew home to Houston. His father was running for the U.S. Senate, and George spent most of the summer riding across Texas in a bus called the "Bush Bandwagon." He worked hard campaigning for his father, meeting people, smiling, and shaking hands. (The elder Bush lost the election that November.)

That fall, George W. moved back east to Yale University. Again, he was following his father's path. Like

George W. Bush attended Yale University from 1964 to 1968. He graduated with a degree in history.

he had at Andover, George W. earned average grades but made a huge amount of friends around the campus. He even joined a fraternity called Delta Kappa Epsilon, and a secret society called Skull and Bones—an exclusive group of which his father has also been a member.

▶ Personality

"Everybody knew George and George knew everybody," said Clay Johnson, a classmate at both Andover and Yale. "People just wanted to be around him . . . And this is before the name George Bush was known."[3]

Though he had now spent quite a bit of time living and learning in the Northeast, he never lost the spirit of his Texas roots. Karl Rove, a friend of the Bush family and political advisor, once had this to say about George W. Bush:

"He is clearly the wild son . . . part of it is rooted in Midland (Texas), where he grew up in an ordinary neighborhood, where houses are close together and risk was a way of life."[4]

Chapter 3 ▶

Business and Baseball, 1968–1989

Politics is the Bush family business. When George W. was a student, his grandfather, Prescott Bush, was a United States senator from Connecticut.

When George W. was an adult, his father was a congressman, the head of the Central Intelligence Agency (CIA), vice president, and finally, president.

▶ George W. Arrived Late at the Family Trade

After his 1968 graduation from Yale, Bush entered what he called his "nomadic period," meaning he drifted from job to job.[1] He spent brief time on active duty as a pilot in the Texas Air National Guard and then he returned to college—this time Harvard University—for his MBA degree. After that, he returned to Texas as a

At the time of George W.'s ▶ graduation from Yale, the Vietnam War was being fought in Southeast Asia. While many other young men were being drafted, George W. was able to avoid this by joining the Texas Air National Guard. He served there from 1968 to 1973.

twenty-nine year old seeking his place in the world. During this time, Bush said, he had to "reconcile who I was and who my dad was, to establish my own identity in my own way."[2]

It was a time of figuring out his place in life, though there was also time for plenty of golf, tennis, dating, and drinking. In fact, during the presidential campaign of 2000, he admitted he drank too much at that stage in his life, but he said he quit when he turned forty and became a born-again Christian. "Drinking began to compete with my energy," he said about his decision to quit. "I'd be a step slower getting up."[3]

▶ Meeting Laura

Another thing that helped settle him down was meeting Laura Welch, a school librarian, in 1976. A couple named Jan and Joe O'Neill was friends with both Laura and George and had wanted the two to meet. Laura, who was on the shy side, continually said no. Eventually she gave in and met Bush during a barbecue at the O'Neill's Midland, Texas, home. George's first impression was that she was "Gorgeous, good-humored, quick to laugh, down-to-earth, and very smart."[4]

George and Laura, who had grown up in the same neighborhood but never met as children, were engaged within months. They were married in November 1977, took a brief honeymoon in Mexico, then returned home to embark on an entirely different adventure.

▶ Candidate for Congress

During the 1970s, Bush's father gained a great deal of political power. He was a congressman, chairman of the Republican National Committee, U.S. ambassador to China, and director of the CIA.

Tools   Search   Notes   Discuss   Go!

Polish State Visit, July 17-18, 2002 - Microsoft Internet Explorer

File   Edit   View   Favorites   Tools   Help

Address http://www.whitehouse.gov/president/statevisit/02.html   Go

• Laura Bush's
  Biography

Speeches
• Speeches by Date
• Speeches by Topic

**Education
Initiative**
• Ready to Read,
  Ready to Learn
• Summary
• Initiative Overview
  (pdf)
• Early Childhood
• Teachers
• Recommended
  Reading

Photos
• Photo Index

**Life at the White
House**
• Behind the Scenes
• Recipes

History
• East Wing History
• Past First Ladies

Photographs & Photo Essays of Laura Bush

Polish State Visit, July 17-18, 2002

Mrs. Bush and Mrs. Kwasniewska stand together during the South Lawn ceremony at which the national anthems for both countries were performed and their husbands reviewed the troops. White House photo by Susan Sterner.

Essay Index
Main Photo Index

Internet

Laura Bush (right) stands with Jolanta Kwasniewska, Poland's first lady, on the South Lawn of the White House in the summer of 2002.

Ever since the younger George Bush had graduated from Harvard and moved back to Texas, he had toyed with the idea of running for political office, too. The opportunity to run for the nineteenth congressional seat in Texas came up right around the time he married Laura.

Shortly after the wedding, George and Laura Bush began campaigning heavily. He was accustomed to shaking hands and giving speeches. Laura—being shy—was not. Sometimes campaigning was stressful.

George Bush won the Republican primary but lost the general election to Kent Hance, a Democrat. Incredibly disappointed, Bush focused on building his oil career.

The same year he was married, Bush had pulled fifteen thousand dollars from his trust fund and set up Arbusto Energy. (Arbusto means "bush" in Spanish.) The oil business went downhill in the 1980s when prices fell. He eventually sold his remaining interests in the business and got out.

A New Line of Business

When Ronald Reagan became president in 1981, George Herbert Walker Bush was his vice president. After George W. Bush got out of the oil business later that decade, he concentrated on his father's campaign to be the Republican presidential nominee in 1988.

By now, George and Laura Bush had a family. (Their twin girls, Barbara and Jenna—named after their grandmothers—had been born in 1981.) Bush moved his family to Washington, D.C., where he worked as an adviser and speechwriter. "I was a loyalty enforcer and a listening ear,"

Barbara (left) and Jenna (right) were born on November 25, 1981.

Tools   Search   Notes   Discuss   Go!

A friendly game of horseshoes at a family picnic. When George H. W. Bush ran for president in 1988, George W. worked as an advisor and speechwriter for his father's campaign.

he said about his role. "When someone wanted to talk to the candidate but couldn't, I was a good substitute; people felt that if they said something to me, it would probably get to my dad. I did only if I believed it was important for him to know. A candidate needs to focus on the big picture, his message and agenda, and let others worry about most of the details."[5]

After his father's election, Bush and his family returned to Texas in 1989. George W. had received a call from his friend, Bill DeWitt, telling him that the Texas Rangers baseball team was up for sale. Bush had always loved baseball, and owning a major-league team would be a dream come true. Back in Texas, he visited the owner, Eddie

Chiles, who also happened to be a well-known Republican and longtime Bush family acquaintance.

There was a problem—a big problem: The Texas Rangers cost $86 million. Bush did not have nearly that much money, but that was not going to stop him. "I had knocked at the door," he wrote in his autobiography, "and I would keep on knocking."[6]

Bush began calling rounds of friends, convincing them to join his purchasing group and invest money in the team. He met a rich businessman from Dallas/Fort Worth named Richard Rainwater, who was also interested in buying the team. Bush and Rainwater joined their groups together and completed the purchase.

Bush's financial share in the team was relatively small—he had invested $606,000, giving him 2 percent ownership. Along with an investor named Rusty Rose, Bush was responsible for the day-to-day management of the franchise. He was a full-time baseball man.

Bush was a popular speaker at various functions and stayed out of the owner's box at games to watch from the stands with the fans. "I want the folks to see me sitting in the same kind of seat they sit in, eating the same pop-corn," he explained to a reporter from *Time* magazine in 1989.[7]

This would seem to be a happy time in Bush's life. His father was president, and he was running a baseball team. Within four years, President Bush lost the White House to Bill Clinton. That ended his political career. For George W. Bush, however, it was a beginning.

Chapter 4 ▶

His Own Political Career, 1994–2000

After President George Bush lost his reelection bid in 1992 to Bill Clinton, George W. Bush felt free to step out of his father's shadow and pursue his own political career. His partial ownership and role as spokesman for the Texas Rangers baseball team had made him a popular public figure in Texas. It also showed that he had sound leadership skills and could run a successful organization.

▶ The Run for Governor

Bush decided to enter the race to be governor of Texas in 1994. As the Republican nominee, he faced a tough opponent in feisty incumbent Ann Richards, a popular governor who was often quoted in the press and seen in the national spotlight.

At the start of the campaign, many did not think George W. Bush stood a chance. Richards charged that Bush was trying to get by on his father's name. Bush replied that he had all of his father's enemies "and one-half of his friends."[1]

George W. Bush was inaugurated as governor of Texas in 1995. He was reelected in 1998.

That was true. Anyone who did not like President George Bush tended to doubt his son. Still, George W. Bush knew how government worked, and he believed he could do the job. "I've got confidence in my capabilities," Bush said at the time. "I love to be underestimated."[2]

An Election Night Victory

Although he was the underdog in the race—Texas, after all, had only one Republican governor since the nineteenth century—Bush won 54 percent of the vote to beat Richards. There were several things that helped: First, he had amassed the most campaign money in Texas history; and secondly, while Richards attacked him personally, he stuck to his campaign theme of talking about issues such as education and welfare reform.

Because the governor's powers are limited in Texas, Bush had to reach out to the Democrats who ran the state legislature to push his program through. In fact, that ability to cooperate with the opposite political party was a message he highlighted in his presidential campaign. Gridlock between Republicans and Democrats had troubled Washington all through the Clinton administration.

Presidential Dreams

In 1998, Bush was re-elected as governor. Soon afterward, he announced his plans to run for president in 2000. Partly because he had amassed a lot of support from Republican Party leaders and because he had a lot of money from donors, many Republican challengers dropped out of the race early. Bush easily won the Iowa caucuses and then got ready to face his major opponent for the Republican nomination: Arizona Senator John McCain.

Bush spent two terms living in the Governor's Mansion in Austin, Texas.

A former Navy pilot and prisoner of war in Vietnam, McCain first challenged Bush in the New Hampshire primary election. McCain's "straight talk" theme worked well and he won New Hampshire. Bush's friends in the Party and the conservative wing rallied in the later primaries and pushed the governor ahead. By March 2000, McCain's campaign was over.

In accepting the Republican nomination, Bush criticized President Bill Clinton and his upcoming opponent in 2000, Vice President Al Gore, by saying: "They had their chance. They have not led. We will."[3]

Bush called himself a "compassionate conservative" and concentrated on several key issues: tax cuts, education, Social Security reform, and returning "dignity" to the White House. By contrast, Gore criticized Bush's record on the death penalty in Texas, the environment, and education. Bush had a huge lead early that began to slip away as the campaign wore on and he had to define what "compassionate conservatism" meant. "It is conservative to cut taxes," Bush explained. "It is compassionate to help people save and give and build."[4]

Polls showed that people believed that Bush was the candidate of change and Gore the candidate of the status quo. Many observers have subsequently felt that the public was tired of eight years of Clinton White House scandals.

▶ A "Supreme" Decision

Although the economy was booming at the time, it turned out to be one of the closest elections in United States history as Bush lost the popular vote but seemingly won the electoral college count. Florida's twenty-five electoral votes were the key. Because it was such a close—and disputed—race in Florida, an automatic recount was necessary by state law. Several weeks passed and Gore's campaign handlers predicted that manual recounts in several key disputed districts would give Florida's twenty-five electoral votes to the vice president. Bush's team sued to stop the recount. Bush was then declared the winner with 49.8 percent of the popular vote and 271 electoral votes. Gore then challenged the result on the basis of reported problems with voting procedures and a flawed certification process. The U.S. Supreme Court, in a 5–4 ruling, decided in favor of Bush.

Weeks after election day, the decision was final: George Walker Bush would become the next president of the United States.

Chapter 5

"Quincy," 2001

When George W. Bush decided to run for president, his father began calling him "Quincy," in reference to John Quincy Adams, the sixth president of the United States. Quincy's father, John, was the second president; together, they formed the White House's first and only father-son combination.

That changed on January 20, 2001, when George W. Bush became the forty-third president. Now, father and son had joined the Adams family in a special place in presidential history.

To tell apart father and son, people who knew both began calling the elder Bush "41," and the younger president, "43." The two presidents began wearing baseball caps with their number embroidered on the front. The new President Bush decided to read a biography of John Quincy Adams. "Ever since the old man called me 'Quincy,' I was trying to find out more about the man."[1]

▶ No Fatherly Advice

Bush's parents stayed in the White House for the first night of his presidency, but his father tended to keep away after that. "I'm going home Sunday," he said a day before his son's Saturday inauguration, "and leave this to Mr. Quincy."[2]

Though both men could relate to the pressures and powers of being president, the elder Bush did not fill his son with advice—not in the White House and not as governor, either. "If he asks for some advice, I would certainly

Online NewsHour: Inauguration 2001 - Microsoft Internet Explorer

File Edit View Favorites Tools Help

Address http://www.pbs.org/newshour/inauguration/index.html

PBS Home   Search   Programs A-Z   TV Schedules   Shop   Membership

Online NewsHour

Inauguration 2001

What's next for President George W. Bush?

- Inauguration Day
- The Speech
- Inaugural History
- Inauguration Fashion
- Presidential Quiz
- Bush Cabinet
- Photo Gallery
- For Teachers
- For Students

home   newshour index   search   forum   political wrap   letters   essays&dialogues   off camera

▲ *George W. Bush was inaugurated as the country's forty-third president on January 20, 2001.*

offer it up," the father told *Newsweek* while his son was governor. "But I'm disinclined (and so is Barbara, in spite of her joking about it) to call up and make suggestions. He knows the number, and knows I'm with him."[3]

The newly-chosen President Bush did surround himself with people who had also served his father. Vice President Richard Cheney was the elder Bush's secretary of defense. Secretary of State Colin Powell had previously served both Presidents Bush and Clinton. Secretary of Defense Donald Rumsfeld, National Security Adviser Condoleezza Rice, and Chief of Staff Andrew Card had all served in the first Bush administration.

Bush also brought with him to Washington his closest aides from Texas, including communications director Karen Hughes and political strategist Karl Rove.

▶ A Dignified Presidency

"Today, we affirm a new commitment to live out our nation's promise through civility, courage, compassion and character," President Bush told the nation in his inaugural address.[4] Seated nearby were his wife and their twin daughters, though Jenna would soon return to college at the University of Texas, and Barbara was headed back to Yale. That left George and Laura Bush to live in the White House residence, along with their dog, Barney.

Just as he had in Texas, Bush habitually went to bed shortly after 9:00 P.M. and woke up before daybreak. He enjoyed reading the newspaper over coffee, walking on the South Lawn of the White House, and taking a morning run.

Inside the West Wing—where the president works— Bush wanted to present a more formal presidency. Both in his campaign and after his election, Bush had pledged to return a sense of character and dignity to the presidency after the scandal-filled years of the Clinton administration. Though he had spent many days during the campaign wearing boots and cowboy hats, the president announced that no blue jeans were allowed in the Oval Office. Staff members had to wear business suits, which represented a serious, dignified presidency.

Things became more laid back when President and Mrs. Bush would visit their ranch in Crawford, Texas, on holidays and vacations. The president spent about a month every summer working from his ranch. To relax, he enjoyed chopping away brush in the woods to make a

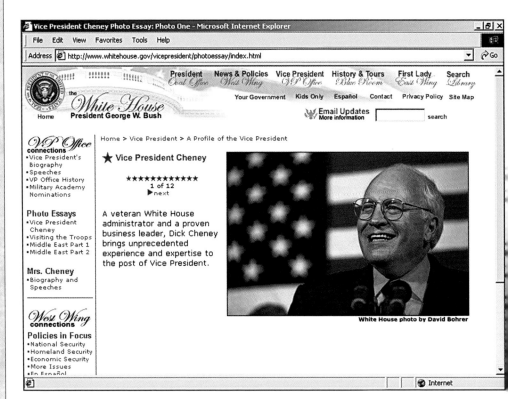

▲ *Vice President Richard Cheney has served four presidents as an appointed official. He had a crucial role as secretary of defense from March 1989 to January 1993.*

path or driving his pickup truck around the grounds while listening to country-western music.

"I recognize the president is in a bubble," he once said, meaning that he is always surrounded by a group of assistants and advisers who want his attention. "But I like to, to the extent that I can, kind of expand the diameter of the bubble. The ranch is a good place to do so."[5]

▶ Money for All

When he first took office, President Bush enjoyed a strong political advantage: Republicans controlled both the House of Representatives and the Senate. With his Party in charge, Bush pushed through one of his major goals: tax reform. In May 2001, Congress passed (and President Bush then signed) a tax-cutting law that sent 98 million rebate checks to taxpayers across the country. Individuals received three hundred dollars; single parents received five hundred dollars; and married couples received six hundred dollars.

"The immediate tax relief will provide an important boost at an important time for our economy," Bush said. "And what is more, is you can feel comfortable using it because more tax relief is on the way."[6]

At the same time that the tax bill was passed, Bush's presidency took a major blow when Senator Jim Jeffords switched his party affiliation from Republican to independent, thus shifting control of the Senate to the Democrats. That slowed down the Bush administration's ability to push legislation through Congress quickly.

During the summer of 2001, economists began noticing signs of an economic recession—a time when prices tend to rise and people do not have the money to freely buy what they want. The nation's money troubles worsened on September 11, when the travel industry (particularly airlines) burst and huge amounts of government money had to be channeled into national defense.

During 2002, stories began breaking about corporate scandals, where the leaders of billion-dollar companies (such as Enron) were found to be misspending stockholder's money. That sent the stock market spiraling downward. At the same time, technology companies (called "dot-coms") that had flourished during the late 1990s were struggling.

First Lady Laura Bush: Inside the East Wing – Microsoft Internet Explorer

File   Edit   View   Favorites   Tools   Help

Address http://www.whitehouse.gov/firstlady/

- Laura Bush's Biography

Speeches
- Speeches by Date
- Speeches by Topic

Education Initiative
- Ready to Read, Ready to Learn
- Summary
- Initiative Overview (pdf)
- Early Childhood
- Teachers
- Recommended Reading

Photos
- Photo Index

Life at the White House
- Behind the Scenes
- Recipes

History
- East Wing History
- Past First Ladies

The Office of Laura Bush

Laura Bush tours the Dwight D. Eisenhower Executive Office Building Library after launching the Executive Office of the President Virtual Library Tuesday, April 8, 2003. "This library is a valuable center of knowledge within the White House. Since it opened 125 years ago, the library has grown from a small reference collection to a modern research facility, with a strong concentration in American history and government," Mrs. Bush said. "Launching the EOP Virtual Library today is a perfect start to National Library Week. This week is not only a celebration of our nation's libraries, but of the people who make them great." White House photo by Susan Sterner.

Laura Bush's Education Initiative

Laura Bush's Speeches
- National Message to the Children of the U.S. Military
- National Library Week Celebration - EOP Virtual Library Launch
- National Library Week, 2003
- **More Speeches and News Releases from Laura Bush**

Photographs & Essays
Mrs. Bush's Photo Index

Initiatives & Projects
Historic Preservation
Mrs. Bush has announced a White House initiative to protect and restore our nation's cultural and natural resources from

Internet

Former schoolteacher and librarian Laura Bush hosted a conference for school librarians at the White House on June 4, 2002. The first lady believes books and information technology aid teachers and parents in students' learning.

By the end of 2002, the United States was stuck in an economic mess. Bush's plan, however, remained focused on cutting taxes.

▶ Everyone Can Read

As a former librarian, Laura Bush made literacy a top priority as first lady. Like her mother-in-law, Barbara Bush, she used her influence to stress the importance of reading. Her husband also made education a top priority of his administration and used the political skills he honed as governor to get it done.

In Texas, Bush had developed a strong relationship with Democrats in the state legislature, knowing it was the only way he could turn his ideas into laws. He found that reaching compromises with Democrats was far more difficult to do in Washington. Bush was able to work with a powerful Democrat, Massachusetts Senator Edward Kennedy, to pass a new education law called the No Child Left Behind Act.

The new law was designed to hold all schools to the same standards, creating strict rules for teachers and principals and giving parents the power to switch their children out of failing schools. "Children respond to an atmosphere of high standards," Bush said in January 2003, one year after the law was signed. "As teachers and parents can tell you, children love to learn, just love it."[7]

The president reaffirmed a promise both he and Mrs. Bush had made when they moved to Washington. "Laura and I share a passion for reading," he said. "We want to make sure every child learns to read by the third grade."[8]

Leading in a Time of Need

When a president takes office, he brings with him a set of goals to accomplish. This is called his "platform"—the ideas he supported and promises he made to get himself elected to the most powerful job in the world.

When George W. Bush entered the White House, reforming education and strengthening the economy through tax cuts ranked among the highest items on his checklist of goals. While education and the economy have been major issues of his administration, both were surpassed in importance by an unexpected challenge—the one that President Bush was given on September 11, 2001.

▶ The Chance to Lead

On the morning of the fateful terrorist attacks, a group of high-ranking Democrats were meeting with members of the media at a breakfast in Washington. Among those Democrats was a man named James Carville, who had helped President Bill Clinton get elected in 1992 and 1996. Carville and his peers were fierce critics of President Bush. During this breakfast meeting, they gave a harsh review of his first nine months in office, calling Bush a weak leader who was unfit to be president.

As the meeting was ending around 9:00 A.M., pagers and cell phones began ringing with the news: Two planes had crashed into the World Trade Center. America was under attack. As people hurried out of the room, Carville called out, "Disregard everything we just said. This changes everything!"[1]

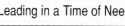
What Carville sensed was that President Bush would now be put in a position of a leader in a time of war. For some time, at least, political arguments would not matter: Americans had been killed, and it was the president's role to console the nation. The country needed to protect itself, and it would be the president's job to make that happen. George W. Bush had been given the chance to be a leader.

A New Checklist

Over the following days and weeks, government agencies and the media pieced together the story of what had happened on September 11. The terrorist group al Qaeda, directed by Osama bin Laden, had launched a coordinated attack on the United States. They trained young men at terrorist camps in Afghanistan and sent them as undercover "operatives" to the United States.

The young men's first job was to blend in as everyday Americans. Some of them were directed to take piloting lessons at flight schools. These men knew that someday they would be called on to carry out a mission. They did not know what—or when—until word arrived shortly before September 11. Believing that they had a religious duty to carry out their instructions, they boarded the airliners and did their deadly deeds.

In response, President Bush directed the United States military to develop a plan for crushing terrorism. He wanted to destroy the training camps and capture the terrorists—dead or alive. He said the United States would "smoke them out of their holes. We'll get them running and we'll bring them to justice."[2]

Now the president had a new checklist—literally. In his desk drawer, he kept a list of al Qaeda leaders, from bin Laden on down.

"I have a classified document that might have some pictures on there just to keep reminding me about who's out there and where they might be," Bush told an interviewer from the television show *60 Minutes.*[3]

Whenever one was captured or killed, he marked it off on the document. "Well, I might put a little check on it, yeah," Bush admitted.[4]

▶ Battle in Afghanistan

The United States' immediate military target was the Middle Eastern country of Afghanistan, which was run by

The United States took military action against Afghanistan after the country's government, the Taliban, would not release al Qaeda leaders to the United States, release all foreign nationals, and close terrorist training camps within the country.

the Taliban government. Under the Taliban's rule, people had few rights and little ability to make their own choices. Men in Afghanistan had to wear long beards, and women could not show their faces in public. The Taliban was an oppressive regime, and worse in America's eyes, it was believed to be protecting bin Laden.

When Bush called for Afghanistan to surrender bin Laden, the Taliban offered to negotiate if the United States could provide evidence of his guilt. The president refused to make a deal. On October 7, 2001, he ordered the first attacks on Afghanistan. The mission was to destroy terrorist camps and overthrow the Taliban, while minimizing any injuries to Afghani civilians.

"More than two weeks ago, I gave Taliban leaders a series of clear and specific demands: Close terrorist training camps; hand over leaders of the al Qaeda network; and return all foreign nationals, including American citizens, unjustly detained in your country," President Bush told the nation. "None of these demands were met. And now the Taliban will pay a price."[5]

During the following months, United States and British military forces successfully removed the Taliban from power. They were unsuccessful in capturing bin Laden, but did play a strong role in setting up a new government in Afghanistan and restoring freedom to the people there.

Long after the fighting stopped in Afghanistan, American troops and spies continued searching for al Qaeda leaders. While bin Laden continued to be elusive, American authorities did capture some of his top aides, including Khalid Shaikh Mohammed, who many believe planned the September 11 attacks.

▶ Homeland Security

While America used its military might overseas, President Bush was also responsible for keeping the country's citizens safe at home. In the weeks following the September 11 attacks, some congressional leaders and members of the media received mysterious mail with a powdery substance inside. It turned out to be anthrax, a deadly toxin. At least five people, including two postal workers, died from sickness after being exposed to the substance.

Americans felt a sense of fear that they had never known. Suddenly, it seemed, air travel was unsafe. Some people felt working in a tall office building was dangerous, too. Now, even the mail could be deadly.

To help citizens feel safe again—and to keep them protected—the government tightened security at airports and on airplanes. For example, all cockpit doors were fitted with locks. A color-coded system was instituted to inform Americans of the threat level for terrorist attacks on any given day. Twenty-two federal agencies were combined in a new Cabinet-level office, the Department of Homeland Security.

▶ An Old Enemy

In 1991, the elder President Bush led the United States through a short but successful war in the Persian Gulf. The Middle Eastern country of Iraq had invaded its neighbor, Kuwait. American forces, with help from European and Middle Eastern allies, forced Iraq out of Kuwait.

The United States stopped short of invading the Iraqi capital, Baghdad, and capturing the country's president, Saddam Hussein. Known to be a brutal dictator, Hussein remained in power over the next decade. Hussein was still ruling Iraq when the younger President Bush took office.

As American officials learned more about al Qaeda, they began to suspect that Hussein had ties to the terrorist network. They also believed that he was concealing weapons of mass destruction. By the middle of President Bush's first term, he decided to attack Iraq and topple Hussein.

Operation Iraqi Freedom

On March 19, 2003, President Bush announced the start of Operation Iraqi Freedom. The United States and Great Britain formed a coalition of countries to invade Iraq. Their goals were to rid the country of all weapons of mass destruction and topple Hussein's regime. Many nations, such as France and Germany, opposed taking military action because they were not sure Iraq had such weapons.

Coalition forces quickly defeated the Iraqi military. On May 1, Bush stated that combat operations had ended. Hussein was captured, and put on trial for war crimes against the Iraqi people. The weapons of mass destruction, though, have yet to be found.

On Monday, March 17, 2003, Bush gave Saddam Hussein forty-eight hours to disarm and leave Iraq or face war. The Iraqi president had ruled the country for two decades as a military dictatorship.

On Wednesday, March 19, 2003, President Bush announced that the U.S. Army was to launch a strike against the Iraqi military in hopes to disarm Iraq and free the Iraqi people from Saddam Hussein's rule.

▶ Reelection

In the election of 2004, Bush faced off against Democratic challenger John Kerry. In a fairly close election, Bush defeated Kerry, a senator from Massachusetts. Bush quickly got back to the challenges of securing a peaceful future for the American people and resolving the situations in Iraq and Afghanistan.

The autumn of 2005 brought a new crisis to the Bush administration. The city of New Orleans and the surrounding area was devastated by Hurricane Katrina. President Bush and the Department of Homeland Security were harshly criticized for the way they responded to the tragedy.

In Spring 2006, United States soldiers were still dying in Iraq and Afghanistan. Osama bin Laden had not been captured. Polls showed that people's support for the war in Iraq was waning. President Bush claims that progress is being made in Iraq and as soon as the Iraqi Army is strong enough, American soldiers will start coming home. Solving these problems are challenges that President Bush will accept. He has been given the opportunity to lead people in a time of true need.

Chapter Notes

Chapter 1. A Day Like No Other, September 11, 2001

1. *60 Minutes* (CBS TV show), September 11, 2002, transcript: <http://sixtyminutes.ninemsn.com.au/sixtyminutes/stories/2002_09_15/story_685.asp> (April 23, 2003).

2. Bill Sammon, *Fighting Back* (Washington, D.C.: Regnery Publishing, Inc., 2002), p. 83.

3. Ibid., p. 90.

4. George W. Bush, "President's Remarks," Emma E. Booker Elementary School September 11, 2001 <http://www.sarasota.k12.fl.us/emma/9.11.01/remarks.html> (April 23, 2003).

5. George W. Bush, "Statement by the President in His Address to the Nation," The White House, September 11, 2001, <http://www.whitehouse.gov/news/releases/2001/09/ 20010911-16.html> (April 23, 2003).

6. Ibid.

Chapter 2. Successful Young Family, 1946–1964

1. Barbara Bush, *Barbara Bush: A Memoir* (New York: Scribner, 1994), p. 42.

2. George W. Bush, *A Charge to Keep* (New York: Perennial, 1999), p. 15.

3. Louis Romano, "George Walker Bush, Driving on the Right," *Washington Post,* September 24, 1998, p. B01.

4. Bruce Partain, "George W. Bush: The Sky's the Limit," *Midland, Texas Chamber of Commerce*, n.d., <www.midlandtxchamber.com/midland/start_files/bush/bush.htm> (May 28, 2003).

Chapter 3. Business and Baseball, 1968–1989

1. The Associated Press, "George W. Bush: Easy to Underestimate," *USA Today Elections,* June 8, 2000, <http://usatoday.com/news/e98/profilebush.htm> (April 23, 2003).

2. Ibid.

3. Ibid.

4. George W. Bush, *A Charge to Keep* (New York: Perennial, 1999), p. 79.

5. Fred I. Greenstein, *The Presidential Difference; Leadership Style From FDR to Clinton* (Princeton, N.J.: Princeton University Press, 2000), p. 276.

6. Bush, p. 199.

7. "George W. Bush," *AskMen.com,* 2000, <http://www.askmen.com/men/business_politics/34_george_w_bush.html> (April 23, 2003).

Chapter 4. His Own Political Career, 1994–2000

1. Cable News Network, "Victory Restores Bush Dynasty to Washington," *Election 2000,* <http://www.cnn.com/2000/ALLPOLITICS/stories/12/13/president.bush/index.html> (April 23, 2003).

2. The Associated Press, "George W. Bush: Easy to Underestimate," *USA Today Elections,* June 8, 2000, <http://usatoday.com/news/e98/profilebush.htm> (April 23, 2003).

3. "Victory Restores Bush Dynasty to Washington."

4. Jeffrey Pascoe, "Vermont Republican Party 41st Annual Dinner with special guest George W. Bush," *Vermont Republican Party*, <http://www.vertmontgop.org/bush1022.htm> (April 23, 2003).

Chapter 5. "Quincy," 2001

1. Judy Keen and Mimi Hall, "'I'm ready,'" *USA Today*, January 12–14, 2001, pp. 1A, 12A.

2. Frank Bruni, "Triumph for Father and Son, and a Wellspring of Feeling," *New York Times*, January 21, 2001, pp. 1, 13.

3. PR Newswire Association, "Newsweek: Interviews: Former President George Bush Texas Governor George W. Bush," *PRNewswire*, June 14, 1999, <http://www.findarticles.com/cf_0/m4PRN/1999_June_14/54865822/print.jhtml> (April 23, 2003).

4. George W. Bush, "President Bush's Inaugural Address," *The White House*, January 20, 2001, <http://www.whitehouse.gov/news/inaugural-address.html> (April 23, 2003).

5. Judy Keen, "Bush says ranch offers him refuge, freedom," *USA Today*, Aug. 22, 2001, p. 8A.

6. George W. Bush, "Remarks by the President on Tax Cut Plan," *The White House*, Feb. 5, 2001, transcript, <http://www.whitehouse.gov/news/releases/20010205.html> (April 23, 2003).

7. George W. Bush, "President Bush Celebrates First Anniversary of No Child Left Behind," *The White House*, January 8, 2003, <http://www.whitehouse.gov/news/releases/2003/01/20030108-4.html> (April 23, 2003).

8. Ibid.

Chapter 6. Leading in a Time of Need

1. Bill Sammon, *Fighting Back* (Washington, D.C.: Regnery Publishing, Inc., 2002), p. 81.

2. Bob Kemper, "Bush asked to tone down war rhetoric," *Chicago Tribune Online*, September 19, 2001, <http://www.chicagotribune.com/news/nationworld/chi-0109190252sep19.story> (April 24, 2003).

3. *60 Minutes* (CBS TV show), September 11, 2002, transcript: <http://sixtyminutes.ninemsn.com.au/sixtyminutes/stories/2002_09_15/story_685.asp> (April 23, 2003).

4. Ibid.

5. George W. Bush, "Presidential Address to the Nation," *The White House*, October 7, 2001, <http://www.whitehouse.gov/news/releases/2001/10/20011007-8.html> (April 23, 2003).

Further Reading

Gormley, Beatrice. *President George W. Bush: Our Forty-Third President.* New York: Aladdin Paperbacks, 2001.

Marquez, Heron. *George W. Bush.* Minneapolis: Lerner Publishing Group, 2001.

McNeese, Tim. *George W. Bush: First President of the New Century.* Greensboro, N.C.: Morgan Reynolds, Inc., 2002.

Ryan, Patrick. *George W. Bush.* Edina, Minn.: ABDO Publishing Company, 2001.

Schuman, Michael A. *George H. W. Bush.* Berkeley Heights, N.J.: Enslow Publishers, Inc., 2002.

Wheeler, Jill C. *September 11, 2001: The Day That Changed America.* Edina, Minn.: ABDO Publishing Company, 2002.

————— . *George W. Bush.* Edina, Minn.: ABDO Publishing Company, 2002.

Wukovits, John F. *George W. Bush.* Farmington Hills, Mich.: Gale Group, 2000.

Young, Jeff C. *Operation Iraqi Freedom: A MyReportLinks.com Book.* Berkeley Heights, N.J.: MyReportLinks.com Books, 2003.

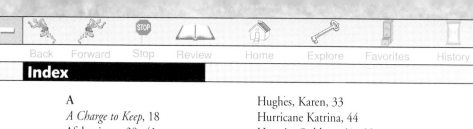